Play Date

by Rosa Santos
Illustrated by Gioia Fiammenghi

The Kane Press
New York

Book Design/Art Direction: Roberta Pressel

Library of Congress Cataloging-in-Publication Data

Santos, Rosa.
    Play date/by Rosa Santos; illustrated by Gioia Fiammenghi.
      p. cm. — (Math matters.)
    Summary: Ivy and Jessica's play date must be postponed again and again until finally, a week after it was originally planned, they are able to get together.
    ISBN 1-57565-105-X (pbk. : alk. paper)
    [1. Days—Fiction. 2. Family life—Fiction.]
  I. Fiammenghi, Gioia, ill. II. Title. III. Series.
PZ7.S23862 Pl 2001
[Fic]—dc21   00-043816
                                                CIP
                                                 AC

10 9 8 7 6 5 4 3 2

First published in the United States of America in 2001 by The Kane Press.
Printed in Hong Kong.

MATH MATTERS is a registered trademark of The Kane Press.

One spring day Jessica met her friend Ivy at the bus stop.

"Let's have a play date," said Ivy.

"I have my tuba lesson today," Jessica said. "How about tomorrow?"

"Okay!" said Ivy.

BUS STOP

Jessica played a new song for her tuba teacher. It was called "June is Bustin' Out All Over."

Jessica's cat, Groucho, hid in the attic.

Ivy played catch with her brother, Otto.

 TUESDAY

When Jessica got home from school the next day, her mother was waiting.

"We have to take Groucho to the vet," she said. "I think he swallowed his toy mouse."

"Poor Groucho!" said Jessica. "But
Mom, what about my play date with Ivy?"
"Sorry, honeybun," said Mrs. Daly.
"Call her and change it to tomorrow."

Doctor March examined Groucho.

"There's nothing to worry about," he said. "It's probably just an upset stomach. Leave him here until tomorrow, and I'll keep an eye on him."

"Tomorrow is Wednesday, isn't it?" said Jessica.

"That's right," said Doctor March. "All day."

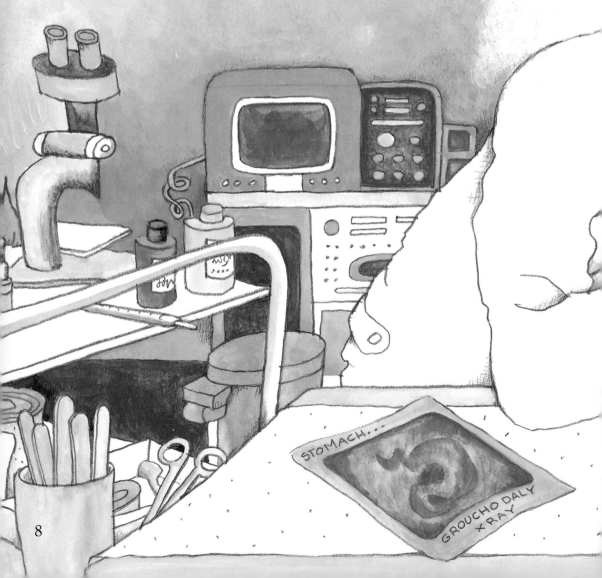

STOMACH...

GROUCHO DALY X RAY

8

When Ivy got home from school on Wednesday, her mother met her at the door.

"Guess who's here!" she said. "Aunt Trudy and your cousins—April, May, and June!"

"Oh, no!" thought Ivy.

April stuck her tongue out at Ivy.

May pulled Ivy's left arm. "Play house with me!" she whined.

June pulled Ivy's right arm. "Play catch with me!" she yelled.

"Mom!" said Ivy. "I have a play date with Jessica today."

"Sorry, sweetie pie," said Mrs. Clarke. "Call her and change it to tomorrow."

When she got off the phone, Ivy played
house with April and May.

Otto played catch with June.

Then everybody played hide-and-seek.
Ivy hid in the attic with Otto. April,
May, and June couldn't find them.

Jessica went to Doctor March's office to
pick up Groucho. He was very grouchy.

THURSDAY

On Thursday, just after Ivy came home, the phone rang. It was Jessica.

"Are you coming over for our play date?" asked Ivy.

"I can't," moaned Jessica. "I'm sick."

"Oh, no!" said Ivy. "What's wrong?"

14

"Mom thinks it's a 24-hour flu," said
Jessica. "I should be better tomorrow."

"Then we can have our play date,"
said Ivy.

"I hope so," said Jessica.

Ivy made a card. She wrote, "Get well soon. P.S. Say hi to Groucho for me." She put it in Jessica's mailbox.

Groucho kept Jessica company. They
both liked Ivy's card.

FRIDAY

On Friday Jessica called Ivy.
"Guess what?" she said. "I'm better!
We can have a play date."

"We can't," croaked Ivy. "Now *I'm* sick!"

"Oh, no!" said Jessica. "Is it the flu?"

"I guess so," said Ivy. "I think it's the same one you had—the 24-hour kind."

"That means you'll be better tomorrow," said Jessica. "Maybe then we can play."

"Maybe," said Ivy. "I'll call you."

Jessica made a get-well card. She wrote,
"Feel better soon. P.S. Groucho says hi."
She put it in Ivy's mailbox.

Otto brought Ivy a plant.
Mrs. Clarke gave her ginger ale and pretzels.
Mr. Clarke read her a story.
Ivy began to feel better.

On Saturday Ivy felt fine, so she called Jessica. There was no answer. Ivy left a message.

"Hi, Jessica," she said. "I'm all better. I was hoping we could finally have our play date today, but you're not home! This makes six tries—almost a week! Call me when you can, okay?"

23

A little later, Ivy and Otto helped their mother in the garden.

Otto picked daffodils.

Ivy cleaned up the flower beds. "When will the tulips bloom?" she asked.

"In about four weeks," said Mrs. Clarke.

"I wonder if I'll have a play date with Jessica before then," said Ivy.

"Of course you will," said her mother.
"That's a whole month from now."
Then the phone rang.

"Hello?" Ivy said.

"Got your message," said Jessica. "Can we have our play date tomorrow?"

"Sure," said Ivy. She thought for a moment. "Unless you have to go to the vet, or my cousins drop in, or one of us is sick."

"Let's cross our fingers," said Jessica.
"My house okay?" asked Ivy.
"Deal," said Jessica. "See you tomorrow."

Jessica was eating breakfast with her fingers crossed when the phone rang.

"Oh, hello, Ivy," said Mrs. Daly. "Of course! I'll tell her. Goodbye."

"Is our play date off again?" asked Jessica.

"No, Ivy just wanted to make sure you were coming," said Mrs. Daly.

Jessica heaved a sigh of relief.

Then her mom dropped her off at
Ivy's house.

When Ivy came to the door she was holding something small and gray and fluffy.

"Surprise!" she said. "Meet my new kitten."

"Eeee!" squeaked the kitten.

"She's so cute!" said Jessica. "What's her name?"